The

Rumor

Trouble on El

Monique Felix

Home foreclosures, the epidemic spawned by the crash of the real estate market, are once ... a potential election-year ...

...rm elections near-...oups and elec-...he country ...owners ...

MR. NORTON said the experience taught him how social networking could be "productive, not just pointless chatter." The founding of Crowdrise sought to enable anyone to do what Mr. Norton did, and to make new friends in the process.

The site, which is run not as a non-profit but as a business, takes less than 8 percent of total money donated, including about 2 percent for credit card fees. "We need serious scale to make this business work," Robert Wolfe said. "But we're in this for the long haul." The actor Seth Rogen is using Crowdrise to raise money to fund research of Alzheimer's disease. Flea, the bassist for the Red Hot Chili Peppers, is trying to build support for basic music education for young people.

But the Crowdrise team is as excited ... — people like ...nfamous users — ...work ...ated ...tion wi... ...or operate ...beds locate...

31: Rehabilita-...viding services ...er County, has a...ill acquire, constr...e project, of appro...$294,930. PROJECT...community residen...New York, New Y...at Yeshiva Univer...atment programs ...and serving appl...ECT 10-OASAS...s) for use a...120 consumers...AS-1091: Beha...ence providi...Clinton Cou...

Conspiracy

ary ho...o place. ...voting is prob-...l thing that's on ...t now," said Rob-...n, president of Fair...

trongest Security

more than four sequential characters from the previous seven passwords, and a new password is required every 120 days.

By contrast, Amazon has only one requirement: that the password be at least six characters. That's it. And hold on to it as long as you like.

A short password wouldn't work well if an attacker could try every possible combi-nation in quick succession...

...ley and Mr. Flore...
...sites can block "br...
...failed log-in attempts...
...locked for 24 hours af...
...tempts," they write, ...
...thstand 100 years of s...
Roger A. Safian, a seni...
...st at Northwestern, s...
...on, the university is u...
...able to brute-force att...
...lock out accounts afte...
...reason, he says, is that...
...a lockout policy to try...
...account, "knowing that...
...owing that the victim...
...nt, either." (Such thou...
...nt facing an un...
...essor of law...

Dozens Killed In Attacks

Strongest Security (M)

Published in 2011 by Creative Editions
P.O. Box 227, Mankato, MN 56002 USA
Creative Editions is an imprint of
The Creative Company.
Designed by Rita Marshall

Printed in Italy

**Library of Congress
Cataloging-in-Publication Data**
Felix, Monique. The rumor / written and
illustrated by Monique Felix.
Summary: News travels quickly through
a small village when a wolf is seen in the
hills, compelling animal friends to warn
one another and, in the process, turn
hearsay into an increasingly inaccurate
rumor. **ISBN 978-1-56846-219-6**
[1. Gossip—Fiction. 2. Communication—
Fiction. 3. Animals—Fiction. 4. Neighbors—
Fiction.] I. Title.
PZ7.F3358Ru 2011   [E]—dc22
2010028645   CPSIA: 120110 PO1408
First edition
9 8 7 6 5 4 3 2 1

Lost in The Dust?

From Page I

...those three foreclosure divisions in Broward than to any other di-...vision in the building in terms of ...managers and that sort of ...to help the general public," ...said. "The people who come ... In any event, huge numbers of ...et fully, fully heard."

...y children getting ...drugs too soon," ...fessor of clinical ...esearcher in the ...study ...

e Side ... ou On

The
Rumor

Monique Felix

Creative Editions

There once was a small,
quiet village built upon green hills.

It was a peaceful place,

filled with good neighbors.

Rupert lived in a house on Cottontail Drive.
There he read the newspaper every morning.
Rupert was so well-informed that he knew what
was happening all around the village.

One morning, **Rupert** read
an alarming report. A wolf had been spotted
roaming the hills! Rupert sprang from his easy
chair and hopped off to warn **Cleo**, who was
napping in a nearby meadow.

Have you heard the news?

A wolf is coming!

They say he has such big ears that he can hear you from a mile   away!

A wolf is

Cleo was so frightened that her fur stood on end. She crept away on the quietest paws to inform **Edgar**, who was watering his garden.

coming!

They say he has such sharp claws

that he can tear your ears into ribbons!

Edgar had always been rather attached to his ears. He tucked them in close to his head and lumbered off to tell **Giselle**, who was painting her house.

A wolf is coming!

They say he has such a strong snout
that he can vacuum you up for dinner!

Giselle imagined how easily she might be vacuumed into such a snout. She dropped her paintbrush and bounded off to alert **Primo**, who was just digging into lunch.

A wolf is coming!

They say his neck is so long that he can strangle you in a knot!

Primo nearly choked on his greens. He grunted nervously and waddled away as quickly as he could to find **Antoine**, who was enjoying a bath.

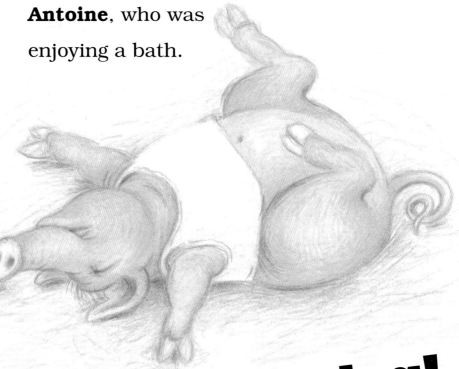

A wolf is coming!

They say he stinks so
badly that you will drop
dead with just one whiff!

Antoine didn't want to get a whiff or drop dead. He splashed out of his tub and crawled off to save **Wallace**, who was gathering wild mushrooms in the hills just beyond his house.

18

A wolf is coming!

They say he has so many teeth that he can devour you in a single bite!

Wallace did not want to be devoured before he was able to eat his mushrooms. So he took his basket into his house and called to his neighbors.

Everybody come inside!

And so Rupert, Cleo, Edgar, Giselle, Primo, and Antoine took shelter in Wallace's house. They double-locked the door, feasted on a delicious mushroom soup, and enjoyed each other's company well into the night.

23

As for
the wolf ...
rumor has it
he still roams
the hills.